D1208312

Rabbi Nosson Scherman / Rabbi Meir Zlotowitz
General Editors

THE STORY OF

Published by
Mesorah Publications, ltd

Chanukah

BY: SARAH LEON
TRANSLATED BY: MICHAL EISIKOWITZ
ILLUSTRATED BY: TOVA KATZ

RTSCROLL YOUTH SERIES®

THE STORY OF CHANUKAH

First edition – First impression: November, 2008

Published by **MESORAH PUBLICATIONS, LTD.**
4401 Second Avenue / Brooklyn, N.Y 11232 / (718) 921-9000 / Fax: (718) 680-1875
www.artscroll.com

Distributed in Israel by SIFRIATI / A. GITLER — BOOKS
6 Hayarkon Street / Bnei Brak 51127

Distributed in Europe by LEHMANNS
Unit E, Viking Business Park, Rolling Mill Road / Jarrow, Tyne and Wear / England NE32 3DP

Distributed in Australia and New Zealand by GOLD'S WORLD OF JUDAICA
3-13 William Street / Balaclava, Melbourne 3183, Victoria, Australia

Distributed in South Africa by KOLLEL BOOKSHOP
Ivy Common, 105 William Road / Norwood 2192 / Johannesburg, South Africa

Printed in Canada
Custom bound by Sefercraft, Inc. / 4401 Second Avenue / Brooklyn N.Y. 11232

ISBN 10: 1-4226-0875-1
ISBN 13: 978-1-4226-0875-3

TABLE OF CONTENTS

A Note to Parents

The Story of Chanukah brings the tale of Jewish determination, victory, and miracles to vivid life for our children. With young Efraim as their guide, they will learn the background, the history, and the lessons of the holiday.

The text, in easy-to-read rhymes that children love, is based on Talmudic, Midrashic, and historical sources, and is divided into eight chapters, one for each night of the holiday.

The graphics are an innovative blend of illustrations and real-life photographs. Sharp-eyed readers will see that there are many images in the pages that come from more modern times and different historical eras. This was done both to add a touch of fun and whimsy, and to make the pictures resonate with the children. We suggest you make the reading experience even more interactive by challenging the youngsters to find these "modern" images that are mixed in among the drawings of the Chanukah era.

Happy reading, and happy Chanukah!

CHAPTER 1 — THE FIRST CANDLE
THE EVIL KING

Shalom, children!
You can call me Efraim.
I've come to you
From the great Chashmonaim.

I've traveled to meet you
From long, long ago,
Here's the Chanukah story
That I want you to know.

In far away Syria
A mighty king reigned.
He was very evil —
We shook at his name!

He was called Antiochus,
So powerful and strong.
"I am great," he said,
"I can do no wrong."

"The world full of people
To my armies they'd fall,
I am the handsome king,
Most powerful of all!''

Antiochus then gave orders:
"Place my statue in each town.
And everyone who passes it
Must bow down to the ground!"

Now all the people in the world
Were terrified, you see;
They didn't dare to think at all —
They bowed down, 1-2-3!

They'd flatter Antiochus
To find favor in his eyes.
"O great and mighty King," they'd say
"You are so very wise!"

But secretly, when no one heard,
In their houses and their huts,
They laughed and said, "It's so absurd!
Antiochus? He's just nuts!"

The Syrian Greeks then came along,
To conquer our land, too
I saw them all from my window,
Loudly passing through.

In their hands they held their spears
And shields down to their knees,
And on their heads wore helmets
That looked like brooms to me!

The soldiers shouted through the town,
"Listen well to the news we bring!
This command is from the crown —
We've come directly from the King!"

"King Antiochus decreed today
A law you must obey.
To his statue you will bow
The time to start is now!"

When the Jews heard this law,
They vowed to remain hidden.
"We'll never serve idols!
We're Jews — it is forbidden!

Though most Jews from among us
Knew which course was right
Sadly, there were very few
Who weren't afraid to fight.

They were very frightened
Their faith, it was too weak.
Others were the Misyavnim —
They copied the Syrian-Greeks.

They dressed in Greek clothing;
From Greeks they bought their shoes.
They didn't do the mitzvos,
And did not act like Jews.

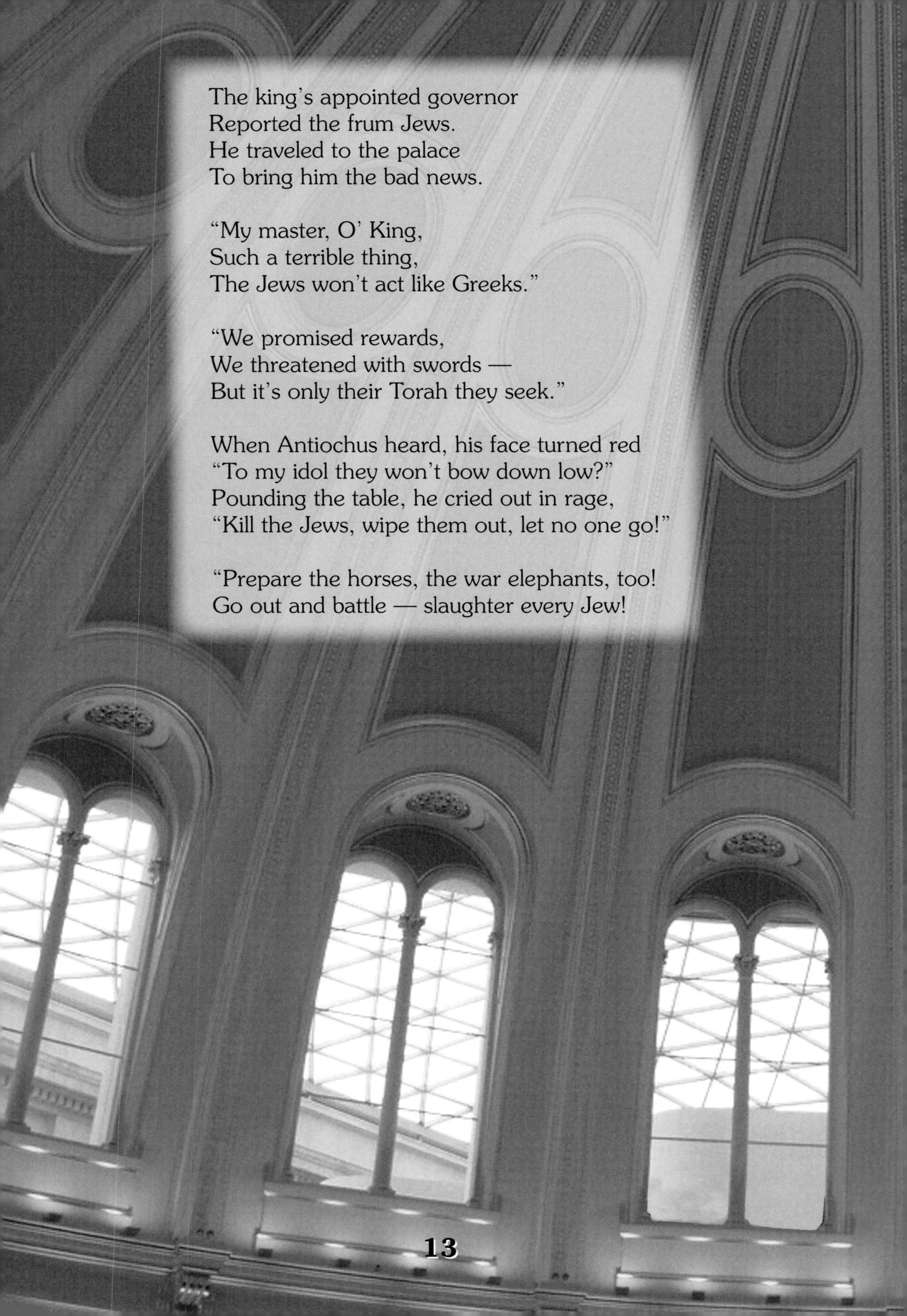

The king's appointed governor
Reported the frum Jews.
He traveled to the palace
To bring him the bad news.

"My master, O' King,
Such a terrible thing,
The Jews won't act like Greeks."

"We promised rewards,
We threatened with swords —
But it's only their Torah they seek."

When Antiochus heard, his face turned red
"To my idol they won't bow down low?"
Pounding the table, he cried out in rage,
"Kill the Jews, wipe them out, let no one go!"

"Prepare the horses, the war elephants, too!
Go out and battle — slaughter every Jew!

CHAPTER 2 — THE SECOND CANDLE
THE SYRIAN ARMY ARRIVES IN ERETZ YISRAEL

The army came into our Land,
And we were so afraid.
We watched the soldiers march on by
With gleaming spears and blades.

To the Holy Temple the soldiers went,
These wicked, evil men.
I closed my eyes so as not to see
What they began just then.

They made holes in the courtyard walls —
BOOM! BOOM! CRACK! so loud!
They ruined the flasks of pure olive oil —
The destruction made them proud.

They set an idol on the Altar
Right in the Temple court.
The holy Menorah from us they stole
And laughed as if in sport.

The Syrians then made wicked decrees —
"Hear ye, hear ye, commands from the King!"
They shouted out loud, "Now listen to these!
Listen well to the news that we bring.

"The great Antiochus
Declared that no Jew
May keep Shabbos, Rosh Chodesh,
And bris milah, too.

"And if someone is caught,
Who dares disobey,
His fate will be death
That very same day."

The king knew that these mitzvos
Are very special tasks —
To make the Jews feel special,
Doing what the Torah asks.

שבת

חודש

מילה

My mother had a baby boy
He's very cute and small
But even though I loved him so,
I wasn't glad at all.

Do you know why I worried?
I would think of him and cry.
How could this baby have a bris?
If they caught us, we would die!

No matter what the Syrians say
A baby boy must have his bris!
So we will do it anyway —
They'll not have their way with this.

We put eight lamps upon the sill
To tell our guests just when
My little baby brother
Would join all Jewish men.

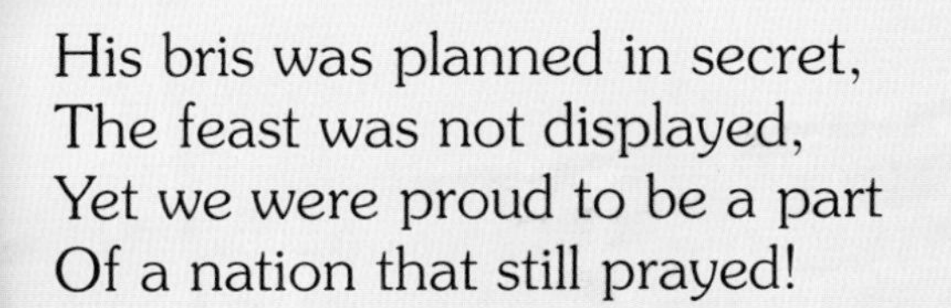

His bris was planned in secret,
The feast was not displayed,
Yet we were proud to be a part
Of a nation that still prayed!

The bris was now done —
Our house filled with joy,
And he didn't cry even once,
This brand-new baby boy.

The baby's named Elazar,
There's a secret in his name —
Hashem will help His people,
He'll save us once again.

The people ate quickly,
And when the time had come,
Each one left in secret.
They slipped out one by one.

CHAPTER 3 — THE THIRD CANDLE
NEW DECREES

The King kept issuing more harsh decrees;
His soldiers traveled all 'round.
When Antiochus sent a new order,
They cried out in each Jewish town:

"Hear ye, hear ye, a command from the King,
Listen well to the news we bring.

"'Carve on the horn of each ox and cow
Large letters that are clear to all eyes,
"In Hashem I don't believe," they'll read,'
Says the king so brilliant and wise."

When my Abba heard this law
He knew what he had to do —
He went out to the marketplace
To sell our cow and oxen, too.

All our neighbors did the same
They sold their cattle, too.
And when the day was over,
You could not hear one "moo"!

"Abba," I said, "without a cow,
There is no milk or cheese for our meal!"
"Abba," I asked, "without an ox,
How can we plow our field?"

I was worried; I was sad.
But Abba, he felt blessed.
"My son, how proud we should be,
Because we passed this test!"

We will not have our cheese and milk,
We will not have our ox or meat,
We proved we believe in Hashem —
That is a most praiseworthy feat!

You can imagine, the king was not pleased;
As his evil decree we did foil!
He thought up another, he just would not stop,
And they said, "In the name of the Royal!"

"Hear ye, hear ye, a command from the King!
Listen well to the news we bring.

"Great Antiochus has made a decree —
Obey it right now, and don't make a fuss.
Write on your doors for everyone to see:
"'Hashem Above does not rule over us.'"

When Abba heard this
He closed up his store.
He went straight to our home
And he removed the door.

Our neighbors — they all did the same
Without complaint or moan,
And when the day was over
There was no door on any home.

I was worried; I was scared
"Abba, we're not safe," I cried.
Nothing will stop robbers
From coming right inside!"

"But we do have a guard,"
Abba said with love.
"Hashem's our protection
From high up above.

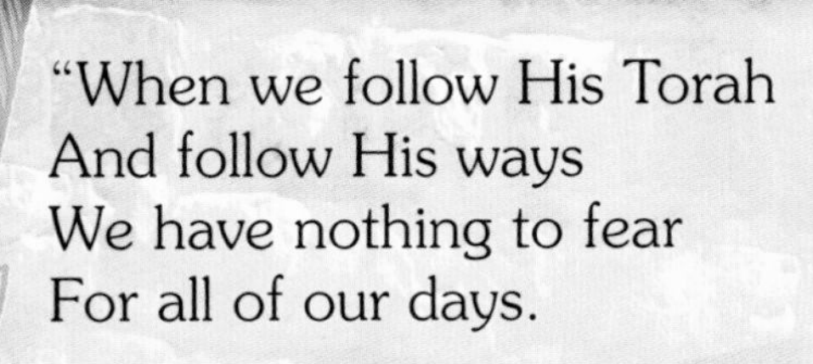

"When we follow His Torah
And follow His ways
We have nothing to fear
For all of our days.

"Our house has no door, but that's fine with me:
It shows everyone who comes our way —
No matter what that bad king will decree
Hashem's are the only rules we obey."

When Hashem saw our deeds
He was really so proud;
He sent us some guests —
There was quite a crowd!

Chickens, deer, sheep, and goats
More kosher birds too!
Our guests made a racket
Our house was a zoo!

The goats gave us milk
Delicious and sweet;
The chickens laid eggs
We had good things to eat!

It was all for the best
That our door wasn't there —
Our guests came right in,
From the ground and the air.

Drop, drip, drop! Do I hear raindrops fall?
In wonderment I scratched my head,
I looked all around and then I saw
A spring bubbling up beneath my bed!

Water, water everywhere,
Gushing from the floor
We don't need a well to draw
Our water anymore!

"Abba, Abba, did you see?
A spring right in our home!"
"Efraim, son, that's wonderful
A mikveh of our own!"

Soldiers had found the mikvaot
And locked them very tight
But now we had our secret place
To do the mitzvah right.

CHAPTER 4 — THE FOURTH CANDLE
NO MORE LEARNING

The king went on oppressing us,
They announced a new decree.
I turned away and closed my eyes;
For I did not want to see.

But that day at the yeshivah,
The iron gate was locked.
Soldiers were there, with glaring eyes —
And me? I just was shocked.

"A new decree," they yelled out loud.
"No Torah — not at all!
Now run along, you can't come in —
Go out and play some ball!"

"What will I do? How will I learn?"
I cried, and ran away.
I love the Torah — I must learn
Each and every day.

The school is locked and guarded,
The shul is closed up tight,
But we continue learning,
Though hiding out of sight.

"Efraim," said my Abba
On one sad gray afternoon,
"My son, you'll have to help me,
We'll be moving soon.

"We'll go to a place
That's very far from here —
Where we can keep the mitzvos
And not have any fear."

We packed up our sefarim,
Our clothing and our pots;
We put them into baskets
And tied them tight with knots.

We put food and water
Right into the cart;
Harnessed our two horses —
We're all set to start.

We only use the side roads
As we find a place to hide.
I wait and wait for it to end,
This long and bumpy ride.

Up the mountains, down again!
We all live in a cave;
Our new home's in the desert —
Now we must be brave.

We don't have a ceiling or floor,
Our home's not large or wide,
But it's filled with light and it's filled with joy
Because we learn Torah inside.

A shelf carved from the wall of rock
Holds all the clothes I wear;
A small stone placed upon the floor
Makes such a cozy chair.

We made a really comfy bed
On the biggest slab of stone.
I have all that I will need
In my brand-new desert home!

Our new yeshivah's in a cave,
And here we come to learn.
We pray and learn the Torah, too,
And with dreidels take a turn.

Yes, dreidel is a useful game
That we play very well,
We use it very cheerfully
In a game of show, not tell!

Our Torah scrolls are gone from sight
When soldiers come to see;
Instead we spin our dreidels,
As if playing merrily.

One day, while learning in the cave,
Quite suddenly we heard
The sound of soldiers' footsteps.
We did not say a word!

Our Chumashim we hid behind a rock —
You know we had no choice;
We took out our dreidels as if to play —
We heard an angry voice.

"Are you studying Torah?
It's not allowed, I say!"
"We're just playing 'spin the top,'
Please join us as we play!"

He entered our cave —
We trembled with fear —
Would he find the sefarim
That were hidden there?

He searched every corner
And poked with his spear.
"Hmmph!" he exclaimed,
"All seems to be clear."

"These kids aren't learning,
Just playing with tops.
Let's go on hunting —
Torah learning must stop."

We waited for a while
In case they would return,
Then took out our sefarim —
There's so much we must learn!

Chapter 5 — The Fifth Candle
The War Begins

One day into the desert
Came a man of strength and might.
His name was Yehudah Maccabbee.
He told us, "Come and fight!"

"Mi LaHashem Ai-lie" he said,
If you're for Hashem, join me —
It's time to fight that evil king,
It's so very plain to see."

Mattisyahu, the Kohen Gadol,
Was Yehudah's father and guide
He yearned to keep the mitzvos
And do all of them with pride.

Mattisyahu had five sons in all,
So righteous and so wise;
They'd lead our Jewish army,
Though it was small in size

We all ran to Modi'in
When we heard this urgent call —
These mighty Chashmonaim
Needed us one and all.

And what did we see
When we came to town?
A soldier was shouting,
"Mattisyahu, bow down!"

They'd set up a huge idol
For people to bow down to
One of the Misyavnim said,
"I will show you all how to."

But Mattisyahu was there
He knew what to do
He broke down the huge idol
And he killed the evil Jew.

The king's soldiers all saw this;
Each one dropped his knives.
They were terrified now
And they ran for their lives!

Antiochus soon heard
He was not very pleased
In fact, he was furious —
"These ...these ... these ... these ..."

These Jews make me angry!
I'll take it no more!"
His temper was flaring —
"We'll go out to war!"

They lined up their great elephants,
And their archers with their bows,
With war horses and their riders,
They were all ready to go.

We, too, prepared to go to war —
We did teshuvah for every sin.
When we do mitzvos and good deeds,
Hashem will always help us win.

The war soon began
The shofar was blown
And we knew in our hearts
We were not alone.

As they came close
The soldiers yelled out loud
"We'll finish them off —
We'll make our King so proud!"

"We've got horses and elephants,
Spears and sharpened knives.
You Jews should be scared,
You should run for your lives!"

CHAPTER 6 — THE SIXTH CANDLE
THE DEFEAT OF THE SYRIAN GREEKS

Yehudah the Maccabee raced to their camp
And attacked their general, the Greek.
The soldiers around him were caught off-guard
They suddenly turned very weak.

The soldiers used bows to shoot at the Jews
But a strange thing happened right then —
The arrows turned 'round, right back they did spin,
And attacked those horrible men.

The soldiers were shocked,
They scrambled in fright,
And then the sky flashed
With lightning so bright.

It struck them like arrows
It made them all blunder,
Then to top it all off,
It started to thunder.

"This isn't natural!"
The soldiers all said then,
"It's their G-d up above,
This comes from Hashem!"

They ran and they ran,
As fast as they could.
They pushed and they trampled —
"We're leaving for good!"

We chased them away,
Right down to the beach.
"We've gotta get out!"
They yelled with a screech.

The men who were left
All swam to their ship.
We called out and laughed,
"Just have a nice trip!"

"Goodbye, I hope you'll all stay away!
Don't ever come back here again!
Instead, go and tell the king in your land
Of the miracles sent from Hashem."

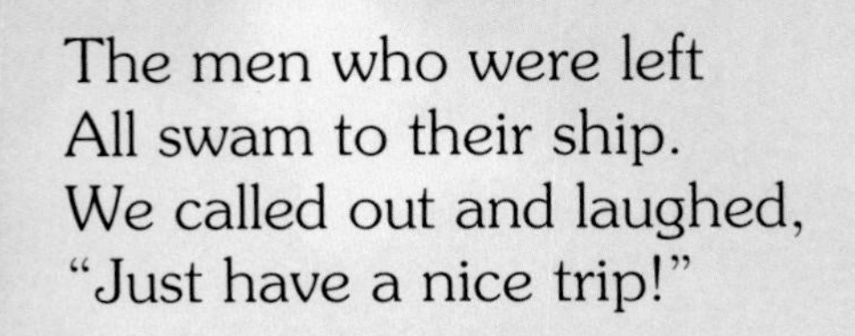

Antiochus, the king
Who had caused all the trouble,
With his carriage he crashed,
It turned into rubble.
His horses went wild,
He fell on his head.
He lay on the ground —
Antiochus was dead.

The nations worldwide
Heard all these great things.
They called out in praise,
They started to sing:
"Hashem rules the world!
He watches us all.
The Jews, they all trust Him —
He answered their call."

The Misyavnim saw what Hashem did,
And all did teshuvah that very same day.
They wore tzitzis, taleissim, and yarmulkes, too,
And the Greek stuff? They threw that away.

CHAPTER 7 — THE SEVENTH CANDLE
THE MIRACLE OF THE OIL

And when the war ended,
We traveled so fast,
To pray at our Holy Temple
That was now free — at last.

But, oh no — look at this!
A terrible thing to see —
Our Temple is in ruins
It just cannot be!

Broken walls and jagged stones
Are scattered all around.
Our Altar's now in pieces,
No Menorah can be found.
Our holy, sacred vessels —
Where did they all go?
The Syrians — they took them —
But where? We do not know.

We needed to clean up
The House of Hashem
So that there He could rest
His Presence again.

We cleaned the holy building,
Threw the idols far outside;
Then built a brand-new Altar
With a ramp that was quite wide.

The Menorah'd been stolen;
We built one anew.
It's important to light it,
'Cause that's what Jews do.

The Menorah, so tall
Was ready — for sure!
But the oil that we found
Was no longer pure.

"What will we do now?"
I said with a sigh,
And then from the floor
A gleam caught my eye.

A jar that's still sealed!
It's just what we needed!
"Oh, Abba, come here!
I think I've succeeded!"

There wasn't too much
Oil in this small flask,
But it was all pure —
What more could we ask?

The menorah was lit,
And to our delight
It just kept on burning
All through the night.

One day, and then two,
Could this really be?
The flames flickered on
To day number three!

Then four, five, and six
Just went right on past;
The lights were still strong —
How long could it last?

When new oil was ready
On the eighth afternoon,
The flames slowly died down,
Not a moment too soon.

"This miracle," said the Sages,
Deserves eternal fame.
A holiday we'll now declare —
Chanukah is its name."

CHAPTER 8 — THE EIGHTH DAY
HAPPY CHANUKAH

Here's a menorah,
It shines very brightly
With cups filled with oil
That we will light nightly.

The lights proudly proclaim
To all who pass by
That the Jews, they live on —
Their flame will not die.

When I see the menorah
I think of long-ago days,
Of Hashem's great, mighty Hand
And miraculous ways.

The soldiers were many
In an army of might,
And our small Jewish group
Didn't know how to fight!

And yet — we beat them
Again and again —
So on each of these days
We say "Thanks" to Hashem.

And now, you and I
Can look at the lights
And remember what happened
On those first Chanukah nights.

One snowy winter morning
Dovid sat in pre-school
He received a menorah
He thought, "This is cool."

"Now where should I put it?"
He looked through his room
"On the roof of my truck;
Through the house it will zoom!"

"Okay, that looks good,
Now everything's right.
I'll drive it around
On Chanukah night."

"Imma, come look!
Imma, come see!
It's a great place!
Don't you agree?"

"My truck — watch it travel
Around and around,
Reminding us all
Of the oil that they found."

"But Dovid," said Imma,
"The menorah must be
High above the ground
So people can see."

"Okay," David thought,
"Where else can I try?
On the bookcase above?
Now that's very high!

"Yes, it's excellent, great,
Now I know where
I'll put my menorah
Right over there."

"But, Dovid, my dear boy,
The menorah must show.
At a window or door —
That is where it must go."

He listened to Imma
And when the stars shone bright
They gathered together
The menorah to light.

The lights twinkled and shone
From the window and door.
A happy Chanukah
For us all is in store.

THE LAWS AND CUSTOMS OF CHANUKAH

▸ **Which berachos do we make when we light the menorah?**

בָּרוּךְ אַתָּה ה׳ אֱלֹקֵינוּ מֶלֶךְ הָעוֹלָם, אֲשֶׁר קִדְּשָׁנוּ בְּמִצְוֹתָיו, וְצִוָּנוּ לְהַדְלִיק נֵר שֶׁל חֲנֻכָּה.

Blessed are You, HASHEM our God, King of the universe,
Who has sanctified us wih His commandments,
and has commanded us to kindle the Chanukah light.

בָּרוּךְ אַתָּה ה׳ אֱלֹקֵינוּ מֶלֶךְ הָעוֹלָם, שֶׁעָשָׂה נִסִּים לַאֲבוֹתֵינוּ, בַּיָּמִים הָהֵם בַּזְּמַן הַזֶּה.

Blessed are You, HASHEM our God, King of the universe,
Who has wrought miracles for our forefathers, in those days at this season.

▸ **On the first day we add another berachah:**

בָּרוּךְ אַתָּה ה׳ אֱלֹקֵינוּ מֶלֶךְ הָעוֹלָם, שֶׁהֶחֱיָנוּ וְקִיְּמָנוּ וְהִגִּיעָנוּ לַזְּמַן הַזֶּה.

Blessed are You, HASHEM our God, King of the universe,
Who has kept us alive, sustained us, and brought us to this season.

After we light the first candle, we say HaNeiros HaLalu as we light the others. Then we sing Maoz Tzur.

- **Why is there one taller candle on the menorah?**

This tall candle is called the shammash. The Chanukah lights are special, so we cannot use their light for anything except for the mitzvah of lighting the menorah. We light a shammash so that if we accidentally use the Chanukah lights, we will have used the light of the shammash, and not the lights of the Chanukah candles.

- **Why do we eat doughnuts and latkes on Chanukah?**

Doughnuts and latkes are fried in oil and they remind us of the miracle that happened when the Jewish people found the small jar of oil that burned for eight days instead of only one day.

- **How many candles do we light on Chanukah?**

On the first night we light one candle, on the second day two, and on each day after that, we light one more candle, until the eighth day, when we light eight candles.

- **What do we use for the Chanukah lights?**

Olive oil is best for lighting the menorah, but any other oil or even wax candles that burn nicely can be used.

- **What does it say on the dreidel?**

There are four letters written on the dreidel: nun, gimel, hay, and shin. The letters stand for the sentence "Neis Gadol Hayah Sham." That means, "A great miracle happened there." In Eretz Yisrael, where the Chanukah story happened, the dreidel has a pey instead of a shin. This combination, nun, gimel, hay, and pey, stands for "Neis Gadol Hayah Po," "A great miracle happened here."

- **Where do we light the Chanukah menorah?**

We light the menorah at the entrance of the house or in front of a window, so that people passing by can see it, or in a doorway inside the house.

- **When do we light the Chanukah lights?**

We light the Chanukah lights after the sun sets, or when the stars come out.

- **What additional tefillos do we say on Chanukah?**

We say Hallel and Al Hanissim.

This volume is part of
THE ARTSCROLL SERIES®
an ongoing project of
translations, commentaries and expositions
on Scripture, Mishnah, Talmud, Halachah,
liturgy, history, the classic Rabbinic writings,
biographies and thought.

For a brochure of current publications
visit your local Hebrew bookseller
or contact the publisher:

Mesorah Publications, ltd
4401 Second Avenue
Brooklyn, New York 11232
(718) 921-9000
www.artscroll.com